A NIGHT AT LETTERS

A Night at Letters

Matthew Kincaide

Matthew Kincaide

1

Son, the county doesn't pay us to send you out on dates! Rob heard his foster father say to him. Rob stepped off the bus. He walked half a block to the bank ATM. He put his ATM card in and punched in his security code. On the screen flashed green numbers, "28.03" Rob pulled out a twenty. This was in addition to the $10 he had in his pocket. He had had a string of waiting jobs, from which he had been fired. Now his unemployment had run out, and he was flat broke. He then proceeded to walk down walked down Santa Monica Boulevard to Letters restaurant. At 6' and 200 pounds, Rob looked like a Greek God. He was very muscular and had chiseled facial features. He looked like a Chippendale dancer. He turned heads wherever he went, and today was no exception. The gay men in the bars all turned to look at him.

Rob did not notice them. He had more important things on his mind. Like how was he supposed to get the rent money by tomorrow morning? Rob had a wife and a three-month-old baby girl to support. He was the chief breadwinner for his family. The pressure was almost more than he could stand. In desperation for money, he remembered one of his gay actor friends talking about Letters restaurant. It was sort of like the Schwabs of the millennium. His gay friend had told him stories of $1,000 "appointments" with old gay men. All you had to do was let these old geysers give you a blow job in exchange for

$1,000. You let these old geysers service you. It was not even like having sex, his friend said. Also, most of these geysers were so grateful that they gladly shelled out another $1,000 for another "appointment. " If you played your cards right, you could easily make $5,000 in a week, his friend said. Rob had dismissed this talk before. However, now that he was desperate, he gave his friend's talk a second chance. I can let an old man give me a blow job. I'll let them have a blow job for a thousand dollars. This will always be a secret. No one will ever know about this. Rob did not know it, but he was about to become "gay for pay" tonight.

Letters was on the second floor of a small building. He walked up to the front door.

He quickly turned down Santa Monica Boulevard and stopped at a phone booth. He put his head against the phone booth and almost cried. I can't do this. I simply cannot do this. What was I thinking of? Yet the gnawing fear of being evicted came back to the fore, and just as quickly, he remembered that he had a responsibility to feed and shelter his family. Even if he could get a legitimate job, it would not pay him money before tomorrow. He was torn and at a crossroads. He could shun Letters, but then he would not have the rent money. This is not to mention that he needed grocery money as well. I'll just walk in and have a drink. That's all-just a drink, he thought.

He turned around and walked back to Letters. Next to the front door was a lesbian bar. It had many women wearing lumberjack shirts. Rob walked up the stairs to Letters. He reached the front door of Letters and walked in. It was completely dark. That was the first thing that he saw was the darkness. Behind the bar were shelves stocked with every possible type of liquor and liqueur.

Five people were sitting in the cocktail lounge. They were fat, pot-bellied, and bald. These were the ugly guys who had to pay for sex. They all looked dejected, sad, and lonely. Rob walked into the bar and immediately turned heads. These old guys were immediately captivated by Rob's beauty. They gave him the once-over looks and wanted to "hire" him for the night. Rob walked up to the bar and ordered a Scotch and soda. He pulled out his twenty dollar bill and paid for his drink. The bartender took his twenty dollar bill and put it under a small light attached to the cash register. Money from young men was always checked for counterfeiting. This bill checked out, and the bartender rang up the sale. The drink cost $10, and the bartender gave Rob two fives for his change. Rob handed one of the fives over for a tip.

Rob sat down at the bar. Rob turned to look out the window. He started hearing voices again. Son, the county doesn't pay us to send you out on dates! He listened to what his foster father said. His foster family took him in solely for the money they would receive from child services. It was worse than a boarding house. More TLC was in a boarding house than in this foster family's home. Rob's foster father was a mean drunk. Every Saturday and Sunday, he would get drunk from twelve-pack cases of beer.

There was another foster child in the family. A girl, her name was Barbara, and Rob just adored her. They got along famously. He was very protective of her. One Saturday, when his foster father got drunk, his foster father punched Barbara in the face and gave her a bloody nose. Rob saw this and immediately went to the defense of Barbara. He punched his foster father and gave him a bloody nose. It turned into a nasty fight, and Rob, who was ten times bigger than the foster father, won. He told his foster father never to touch Barbara again. His foster father would win his revenge, however. The foster father called the police and arrested Rob for assault and battery. The police took Rob away in handcuffs. The foster father was screaming at Rob, telling him he could not return to this house again! The police put Rob into a juvenile detention facility. The district attorney would not prosecute, but Rob had just lost the only family he had ever known. He was on the high school football team. However, there would be no more high school football games. There would be no more dates, no more dances, and no more girlfriends. He would live in juvie hall for the rest of his teenage years.

Rob could never tune out his voice. Wherever he went, or no matter what he did, he heard voices. Rob was an undiagnosed schizophrenic and autistic man. He would listen to voices for the rest of his life and could do nothing about it.

Rob turned to look at the bar. He was repulsed by what he saw—half a dozen of the ugliest and fattest guys he had ever seen. I can't do it with any of these guys, he thought. Then his money problems came to the fore. He looked over at these men again. Maybe, I could let these guys have a blow job? That's all, just let them serve me, he thought. He finished his drink and ordered another one.

Rob had caused quite a stir upon entering the bar. The fat and balled men were immediately taken with him. Even in such a place as this, known for its male beauty, Rob stood out as the most beautiful of the men here. Rob looked down the bar at the old fat men on the other side of the bar. They were giving Rob come hither looks. One of the men was a cancer re-searcher. He was helping in the drive to cure cancer. However, here he was, just one more lonely old troll looking for some human companionship-looking for a warm body to hold him and soothe him. Rob looked at the guy again. No way would I let that guy touch me. He's so ugly it's a crime, Rob thought.

At that moment, two gigolos - Bob and Tom - entered the cocktail lounge. They surveyed the scene.

"Looks like slim pickings tonight," Tom said to Bob.

Tom looked at the bald, pot-bellied men at the bar. Tom did not like servicing or even being touched by old lonely, bald, pot-bellied men. Yet they were his clientele. Young handsome men did not have to pay for sex. They only paid for it for a thrill. So Tom was stuck with these old geysers.

Bob and Tom looked across the room and saw Rob. Rob's handsomeness instantly took them,

"Bob, who's that? I've never seen him before," Tom asked.

"I don't know. I'm goin' over to check him out," Bob answered.

He walked over to Rob and introduced himself. They shook hands.

"I haven't seen you here before. Are you from around here?" Bob asked.

Rob lived in a seedy part of Hollywood.

"Yeah, yeah, I live in Hollywood," Rob answered.

"Is this your first time here? I haven't seen you before," Bob asked.

"Yeah, yeah, this is my first time here," Rob answered.

"What gym do you belong to?" Bob asked.

Rob did not belong to a gym right now, but he decided to lie and say that he was a member of Stone's gym. All the serious bodybuilders went to Stone's gym.

"I go to Stone's gym," Rob answered.

"Me, I go to Seven Day Fitness. I've also had some work done. I had my biceps worked on, and I've had my delts and pecs worked on," Bob said.

Rob needed to learn what Bob was talking about.

"What do you mean you've had work done?" Rob asked.

"I've had silicone implants on my biceps, delts, and pecs," Bob answered.

This took Rob entirely by surprise. Silicone implants!?!, why didn't he work on weights like the rest of us? Rob wondered.

Rob decided to ask about money.

"What do you take these geysers for?" Rob asked.

"It depends," Bob answered, "For an evening, I charge five hundred. I charge a thousand dollars for a weekend trip to Las Vegas. For a weeklong trip to Hawaii, I charge a thousand dollars."

How can you stand to do it with these guys?" Rob asked.

"Oh, I only let these guys give me a blow job. That's all. It's not even like it's sex. All you do is let them have a blow job, and it's an easy five hundred," Bob answered.

I could do that; I could let these geysers have a blow job for five hundred dollars, Rob thought.

Rob, however, was checking out the competition as well. Bob wore heavy Indian jewelry and loud clothes, and his hair reached down to his waist. To Rob, Bob looked like an end-of-the-line gigolo. Clearly, Bob was no competition.

"I'll tell you, though, if you do a couple of gay porn flicks, you can charge a thousand dollars a pop. Me, I want to get into the (entertainment) business. I want to be an actor. This just pays the bills until I make it, and I will make it. I just know it. In the meantime, I'm squirreling my money away. I have ten thousand dollars in a safe deposit box. At this rate, I'll have twenty thousand in six months. Then I'm going to buy a small apartment house and sit back and collect the rent. Then I'm going to buy another small apartment house and build on that. I don't want to let these trolls run their hands up my thighs all my life. I have a plan. I'm going to give you some advice. Stay off the Internet, and don't advertise in the gay magazines. Bob was referring to the classified sections of the gay magazines where there were advertisements for "male escorts" and "masseurs" This is what the vice squad does. They post the classified sections on a wall. Then they throw a dart at the classified section ads. Whatever ad they hit, that's the guy targeted for arrest that month. You'll never make it as an actor if you're convicted of this. Likewise, stay off the Internet. The vice squad hunts us down there, too, The vice squad knows about this place, but they leave us alone here. We're safe here. I've heard some guys get raped doin' this, but hey I can take care of myself," Bob said.

Just then, an adorable blonde boy named Sean walked into Letters. He also turned heads. He was friends with Bob and came over to say hello to Bob. Rob was immediately captivated by Sean. What a cute little Twinkie, Rob thought.

"Bob, it's great to see you," Sean said.

Bob hugged Sean and said it was great to see him too. Then Sean turned to Rob and said:

"Who's this? Do we have new blood around here, or what? I'm Sean," and he held out his hand.

Rob shook hands and said hello.

The Scotch that he was drinking was beginning to have its effect on Rob. He was feeling loose and even a bit happy. He might have taken Sean home if he had not been looking for money. However, Rob had serious problems that had to be taken seriously tonight the need for cash.

"Where do you live?" Sean asked.

"I live in Hollywood," Rob answered.

"Where do you live?" Rob asked Sean.

"Oh, I live in Malibu," Sean answered.

Malibu? That's expensive, Rob thought. How can he afford it? Rob wondered.

"What do you do for a living?" Rob asked incredulously.

"Oh, I don't work. Work is a four-letter word. Besides, work would interfere with spa days," Sean said with mock surprise.

Sean easily commanded $1,000 for just a few hours of "work." At $1,000 a pop, Sean could easily pay his $3,000 a month rent. However, Sean did not need any competition, and Rob was undoubtedly competition.

As they were talking, Tex came into the restaurant. Tex looked like someone right out of Central Casting. At 6' 250 pounds, he looked like the stereotypical Texan. He was wearing a Texan tie and, of course, the Texas cowboy hat. He had a pot belly and looked larger than life.

"Tex's here," Bob screamed.

Sean looked immediately toward the front of the restaurant. Tex was one of Sean's regulars. Sean was a little short and needed an "appointment" with Tex to pay the rent. Both Bob and Sean went over to Tex. Tex was glad to see both of them. Tex said hello to Bob and Sean. They were his regulars. Just then, Tex looked across the bar and spotted Rob.

"Good lord, get a load of that," Tex said as he looked at Rob. Tex had seen much male beauty, but Rob took the cake. Tex was intent on squiring Rob around to Tex's house. Then he asked Bob and Sean who that new guy was at the bar's end.

"His name is Rob; I haven't seen him before here," Bob answered.

"Well, let's go over and say hello," Tex said.

Tex, Bob, and Sean walked over to Rob.

Upon reaching Rob, Tex held out his hand and gave Rob a warm Texas hello.

"Hello, I'm Tex. That's short for Texan. Who are you?"

Rob was taken by surprise by this introduction. He shook hands with Tex.

"Rob...my name is Rob," Rob answered nervously.

"I haven't seen you around these here parts before. Where have you been hiding yourself?" Tex asked.

"This is my first time here," Rob answered.

"Well, it's great to see you here," Tex thundered.

Tex looked at Rob's glass and saw that it was almost empty.

"Who wants a drink? This rounds on me," Tex bellowed.

Bob and Sean asked for drinks. Tex asked Rob what he was drinking. Rob said a Scotch and soda, and Tex ordered four drinks from the bartender and paid forty dollars. Tex paid with two twenty-dollar bills. The bartender did not check Tex's bills. Tex was a good customer and could be trusted. That did not leave enough money for a tip, though, so Tex placed a twenty-dollar bill on the bar for a tip. Tex liked to think he did everything larger than life, and tipping was no exception. The drinks were really taking their effect on Rob. He felt loose and relaxed. He found it easier to talk to Tex.

Tex loved to regale people about his cattle ranch in Texas. He also liked to talk about his trips to Cuba and Thailand. Cuba and Thailand were both sexual Disneylands for adults. Cuba and Thailand both had teenage prostitutes, both male and female, and live sex shows. Tex loved Cuba and Thailand, and he went there every few months. In Thailand, there were gay brothels. On the brothel's stage were a dozen teenage boys in Speedos and numbers in cardboard hanging around their necks. Tex would point out to the bartender which teenage boy he wanted to spend the evening with. Tex and the boy would set a price for the boy when the boy came off the stage. Then he and the teenage boy would go to a private room. He also liked Cuba. Tex said: "You can get any pretty boy you want for a hundred dollars. Giving these boys a hundred American dollars was like giving them gold. These boys will do anything to get their hands on those American dollars,"

However, Tex had never seen such male beauty as Rob in Cuba, Thailand, Texas, or Los Angeles. He was determined to have Rob all to himself tonight. Tex thought that Rob made Bob and Sean look like road kill. They continued to talk and drink for the next hour and a half. Tex bought three rounds of drinks. Rob felt sloshed by four Scotch and sodas. After the fourth Scotch and soda, Rob excused himself to go to the restroom. He threw some water on his face and looked in the mirror. What am I doing? he wondered. How could I possibly do something like this? Then he remembered his responsibility to his baby. He steeled himself and decided to go back and join Tex. He thought he could stomach Tex for one night. Just let this old guy have a blow job, and that's all. He decided to go back and join Tex.

Just then, a sight no one had ever expected to see at Letters happened. A pair of gay twin-brother gigolos entered the cocktail lounge. Everyone stopped and stared at them. No one had ever heard of gay twin brother gigolos, let alone seen them in person. They saddled up to the bar past gawking patrons. They ordered two Budweisers.

"Okay, we hold out for a thousand for each of us," one brother said to the other. Tex was immediately captivated by both of them. He walked over to them, leaving Rob, Bob, and Sean crestfallen and worried about that night's money. He introduced himself to the twins and offered to buy them real drinks, which they readily accepted. Tex considered bringing Rob and the twins to his Bel Air house for a "party." The possibilities seemed endless to Tex. However, he paused when he found out these boys wanted a thousand dollars each. He did not have that kind of cash on him tonight. He decided to make a date with them for tomorrow night. They would have dinner and then go back to Tex's house. Tex went back to Rob.

Then Tex decided to go in for the kill with Rob. "Are you available for an appointment," Tex asked haltingly.

Rob was taken by surprise. He did not want to go anywhere with Tex-free drinks notwithstanding. However, he needed money desperately for the rent-to say nothing about groceries.

"Yes," said Rob nervously.

A wide smile beamed across Tex's face. He slapped his hand on Rob's shoulders.

"Well, that's great, just great," Tex bellowed.

Tex asked Rob what he charged for an appointment. Rob thought for a moment and decided to go for broke.

"I charge one thousand dollars," Rob said.

"Deal," Tex said as he shook Rob's hand.

Bob and Sean felt crestfallen. They also needed money for their rent and groceries too. Now, Rob was stealing the goose that laid the golden egg. Tex put his arm around Rob's shoulders and started for the door.

This is just a blow job. That's all. This is a one-time-only thing. Rob thought I'd get a thousand dollars, and then I'll never return here again.

The fat, bald forlorn men at the bar watched enviously as Tex and Rob walked out the front door. They, too, felt crestfallen about Rob leaving with Tex. They had wanted to go with Rob themselves.

2

Tex and Rob walked outside the restaurant and up to an elevator that took them to the parking garage. The parking attendant brought out a Cadillac Fleetwood Brougham. There were cattle antlers on the hood of the car. The whole car reeked of Texas. They got in the car, and then Tex drove out of the garage onto Santa Monica Boulevard. Tex drove down to San Vicente Boulevard. The gay bars were just getting crowded at 10:00. The sidewalks were teeming with beautiful young boys. At the intersection of Santa Monica and San Vicente, Tex waited for the crowd to cross the corner before he turned right up San Vicente. He drove up to Sunset and turned left towards Beverly Hills.

Son, the county doesn't pay us to send you out on dates, Rob heard his voices say. Please, no voices tonight, no voices tonight, Rob thought. He was nervous as it was, and he did not believe he could control himself.

They drove down about ten miles. They passed Jayne Manfield's famous pink mansion. Tex pointed out the house to Rob.

"That's Jayne Mansfield's house. She had the best damn pair of titties you ever saw. She was as big as Elizabeth Taylor, and Liz had big titties, too," Tex said.

Rob wondered why a gay man would be talking about breasts. Rob did not realize that the men were expected to act like hard-charging, hard-drinking womanizers in Texas. Tex was acting the way he had been raised to act.

A few miles away, they came to the entrance of Bel Air. The streets became narrow and winding as they drove up into the hills. Finally, Tex parked the car in the driveway, and Tex and Rob entered the house. It was a lavishly furnished house. In the living room, above the fireplace, were two cattle antlers. On the wall was a cattle skull attached to the wall.

"Would you like a drink?" Tex asked.

"Sure," Rob answered.

"Scotch and soda, right?" Tex asked.

"Right, Scotch and soda," Rob answered.

Rob was very nervous and was about to talk to Tex about payment for this evening. Then he decided to let it ride for a little bit.

Tex fixed two Scotch and sodas in crystal glasses and handed one to Rob. They both took gulps of their drinks.

"Let's go out by the pool," Tex said.

They walked out the back patio door to the pool. It was placid and aqua-blue.

"Well, maybe you'd like to take a swim," Tex asked.

"I don't have a bathing suit," Rob answered.

"Oh, hell, you can go skinny dipping. The neighbors won't see anything. C'mon, do this for me," Tex said.

Tex was dying to see Rob nude, and this was the best opportunity. Rob decided that if the neighbors could not see him, he would take a skinny dip swim. He took off his clothes and laid them on a lounge chair. Then he dived into the cold water. After a minute, the water felt good. It was cool, but not cold. It was relaxing. Rob needed to unwind tonight.

Tex was taken aback by how beautiful Rob was. He had never seen such beauty before, and tonight Rob was all his. He paid for the privilege, and he was going to enjoy it.

However, Tex had to go to his bedroom very quickly. He excused himself and went up to his bedroom. Upstairs was a handgun. Tex felt the need to protect himself because a couple of months ago, he had picked up another gigolo at Letters. He had brought the gigolo home. When they arrived home, they went to the pool. Then the gigolo pulled out a switchblade. Tex was not carrying his gun then and was forced to go to his bedroom. Tex paid the gigolo a thousand dollars. Then the gigolo pulled out a pair of handcuffs that had been hidden and were hanging from his waist. The gigolo handcuffed Tex to his bedpost. The gigolo started to rifle through Tex's belongings. He grabbed all of Tex's Indian jewelry and demanded to know where more money was. The gigolo went through his pockets when Tex told him no more money was lying around. He pulled out Tex's car keys. Tex begged to be unhandcuffed. Tex told the gigolo that he could take the car, just untie him! The gigolo was not about to let Tex go free. He took his money, Tex's Indian jewelry, and the keys to Tex's Cadillac. Tex was left handcuffed to the bedpost. He would remain handcuffed for three days until his cleaning lady came by to clean the house. When the cleaning lady arrived, Tex screamed for help. The cleaning lady ran upstairs and saw Tex lying handcuffed to the bed. By this time, Tex was sitting in his feces and urine. After he had been cleaned up, he phoned the police and reported his car stolen. It was too late, however. The gigolo had sold the Cadillac to some chop shop. Tex would never see his beloved Cadillac again.

Also, Tex was determined never to be tied up and worked over again. He picked up his handgun, put it inside his belt, and went to the pool. He walked to the edge of the pool. He pulled a thousand bucks in $100 bills from his wallet and placed it on a small table. Rob walked dripping wet out of the pool. The swim had been very relaxing and soothing, making him feel good in connection with the drinks. Rob's nude beauty bedazzled Tex. Tex pulled out his gun and pointed it at Rob. Rob was immediately taken by surprise and scared.

"Hey, look, man, you don't need to be carrying a gun," Rob said.

"Look yourself, young man; you won't do anything to me. There's your money on the table. I don't go cheating, people. But by the same token, I'm nobody's fool, and you won't brutalize me. As long as you do as you're told, I won't shoot you. After you've serviced me, you can take your money and go. I don't care what happens to you after that," Tex snarled.

Rob held up his hands.

"Listen, I'm not going to hurt you. I just want to get my money and leave," Rob said.

"I'm not going to hurt you either," Tex said.

Then he waved the gun at Rob and said:

"This is just a little protection for me. Well, let's get it on like they say in the song," Tex said.

Tex got down on his knees before Rob.

Rob leaned his head back, and a tear flowed down his eye as Tex gave him a blow job.

Afterward, Rob and Tex went up to Tex's bedroom. Tex wanted to put his hands all over Rob's beautiful nude body. Nothing could have disgusted Rob more. Tex put his hand on Rob's chest. Rob flinched. This angered Tex.

"Look, I'll pay you an extra five hundred if you let me touch you and hold you tonight. Let's get into bed and cuddle," Tex said.

Tex disrobed, and Rob saw one of the ugliest bodies he had ever seen-white skin, a sagging chest, a pot belly, and a small penis surrounded by bushy pubic hair. Rob was immediately repulsed by what he saw. Yet for another five hundred, Rob would swallow his disgust and let the old man touch him. They got into bed, and Tex started putting his hands all over Rob. Rob was more disgusted than he could say. He was afraid he would vomit, yet he could do it for $1,500. Tex caressed Rob's chest, stomach, private parts, thighs, and buttocks.

"You're the most beautiful man I've ever seen," Tex said while kissing Rob.

Then Tex did something that revolted Rob even more. He insisted on French kissing Rob! Rob had never been so disgusted in his life. Before he met his wife, he had French kissed other guys, but this was the most revolting thing he had ever done. He had not thought that things could have gone so far.

"I'm so lonely, and you're so beautiful; please stay the night. I need someone," Tex pleaded.

Tex was just a lonely old man paying for love and companionship. However, Rob had a wife to get back to. He could not stay the night.

"Look, I'll stay for another hour. Then I have to go," Rob said flatly.

"Okay," Tex said, grateful for another hour.

They resumed French kissing and caressing.

"I have a great idea. Why don't I take you to Hawaii for a week? We'd have a blast. Have you ever been to Hawaii?" Tex asked breathlessly.

"No, why no, I haven't," Rob answered.

"Good, then it's settled. Next week we'll go to Hawaii, and we'll have a grand time. I want to hold you now and go to sleep," Tex said.

"I can't stay the entire night, I just told you. I'll leave my phone number with you, and I want my extra five hundred," Rob said.

"Go through my pants pocket and pull it out. It's yours. You earned it. Do you need a ride?" Tex asked.

"No, that's okay. I'm good to go," Rob said.

With that, he kissed Tex goodbye and pulled out five hundred dollars from Tex's pant pocket. Then he went downstairs to retrieve his clothes and his one thousand dollars. He dressed and then left. Fifteen hundred bucks for doin' nothin'. How lucky can you get? All he did was let this guy give him a blow job and caress him, and now he was fifteen hundred dollars richer. In just one night, his problems had been solved. Next week, he was headed to Hawaii for another one grand. Life looked like it was getting better.

He went out of the house and onto the street. Rob checked his watch. It was three in the morning. The streets were deserted, and he began to walk down to Sunset Boulevard. He got halfway down when a security guard in a car pulled up alongside him and asked him if he needed a ride. Rob said yes, and he climbed into the car. The security guard drove him to Sunset. At Sunset, there was a convenience store.

Rob walked in and bought a bottle of beer. He paid with one of the one hundred bills he had just earned. The cashier wanted something else. Yet he took the bill anyway. He gave Rob twenty dollar bills in change. With that, Rob decided he could take a cab home. He went in front of the store and hailed a cab. The traffic was all right. At this hour of the morning, few people were on the streets. The taxi drove into Hollywood and deposited Rob in front of his apartment building. Rob walked up to his apartment. His wife and baby were sound asleep, so Rob was quiet. He did not feel tired until he got in the cab. It had been a long and nerve-wracking evening. He had never prostituted himself before, and it sapped him of his energy. The bed looked great to him. He put the one hundred dollar bills on the nightstand next to Sheila. He stripped off his clothes and climbed into bed beside his wife.

Sheila, his wife, woke up around seven a.m. Sheila was an early riser, and Rob was a late riser. Early and late risers always married and tried to change each other. Sheila was a nervous wreck. She had been up since last night. She and Rob fought over money. When he stormed out, she did not know what to do. Not only that, but he had not called her to say where he was. She did not know where he was. She had been frantic with worry over him. At midnight, she had decided that she would go to bed. Now that she was woken up, she had mixed feelings. Her biggest worry was how they were going to pay the rent. She looked over at Rob, sound asleep. She was not going to wake him to talk about the money. Just then, she looked at the nightstand beside her.

There was a stack of $100 bills totaling $1,500. Where did this come from? She thought as she picked up the money. She was not only worried about no rent money, but she was now worried about this money. Was Rob involved in something illegal or illicit? She wondered. She decided to wake him up at the thought of him doing something illegal. She pushed him around on the bed until he woke up. When he had woken up, she picked up the money and asked:

"What's this?" as she held the wad of bills up.

Rob was in a quandary. He could not tell his wife he had been a gigolo last night. Moreover, he had to think up a lie to tell her at a moment's notice. Fortunately, Rob could think of excuses quickly.

"Why that? That's money I earned last night as a waiter," he answered dishonestly.

"A waiter? They paid you in cash?" Sheila asked suspiciously. "What kind of restaurant pays its people in cash?" Sheila demanded.

This was too strange for Sheila. Restaurants did not pay their people in cash. Rob was lying about something. He was hiding something. Her woman's intuition told her so. Rob thought fast on his feet again.

"It wasn't a restaurant. It was a catering service. They want to keep their finances off the books. That's why they paid me in cash," Rob answered.

He needed to change the subject, and he needed to fast. Sheila might find out about his lie, and then what would he do?

I'm going to go to the bank and deposit this money. Then I'm going to pay the rent. Then we're going grocery shopping, and later, I'm going to take you out to dinner. So get a sitter for the baby." Rob said all the while he was desperately trying to keep his secret a secret.

"Rob, you're hiding something from me. No restaurant or caterer pays their people in cash, and especially not this much money," Sheila said.

"I'm telling you it was a caterer paying in cash. They want to keep things off the books. It's all right, I'm telling you." Rob said and kissed his wife on the lips.

"Right now, I could use a cup of coffee and breakfast. I'm starving," Rob said.

This deflected Sheila's suspicions for a minute, and she went into the kitchen to cook Rob's breakfast. However, this was not the end of things by any means. There was something fishy about all this. Her woman's intuition told her that Rob was in some danger. Rob was hiding things from her, and she could not figure something out yet! However, she would get to the bottom of this somehow.

Just then, the baby started crying. Sheila immediately went to the baby. She either needed changing or feeding. Sheila put her hand down on the diaper. She was dry. She needed feeding.

She breastfed the baby. Rob was relieved at the crying of the baby. He never thought that he would be glad to hear the baby cry. However, it deflected his wife's attention away from the money. After she had fed the baby, she put the baby in her bassinet. Then she went into the kitchen and made Rob a breakfast of French toast, Rob's favorite breakfast. She was nervous and skeptical, but having enough money to pay the rent and buy groceries was nice.

After breakfast, Rob quickly dressed went to the bank, and made a $700 deposit to pay the rent. He felt rich peeling off seven one hundred dollar bills. Next, he went to the apartment manager's office and paid the rent with a check. It felt good to have the rent paid. Even though he had prostituted himself to get the money. By the time he returned to the apartment, Sheila was dressed and ready to go grocery shopping. She was holding the baby, wearing the cutest little pink outfit. Rob went over and kissed the baby and then took the baby in his arms. He loved the baby. The baby was the apple of his eye, and he was glad he could now afford the baby. Babies were expensive. They needed shelter, food, clothes, and medical care, which cost money! Rob was not proud of himself for prostituting himself. However, he was exceedingly glad he could now support his wife and baby. Going out that evening was also fun. They had not seen a movie in months. With his newfound cash, he bought his wife dinner and a movie. They considered attending the dance clubs, but the babysitter had to leave at about midnight. They would go out dancing another time, they decided.

When they got home, Sheila told Rob he was not off the hook yet. She was determined to find out where that money came from.

"It was just an off-the-books catering job," Rob said in a bald-faced lie.

Tex called the next day.

"Howdy, pardner. How's my favorite boy toy?" Tex asked.

Rob did not like being referred to as a "boy toy." He would have to have a word with Tex about that.

"Remember our little trip to Hawaii? I made the reservations for tomorrow. Where do I pick you up?" Tex asked.

Rob was taken by surprise. Even though he had given Tex his phone number, he did not think Tex would call so soon. He could not afford to let Sheila hear this conversation. He had to cut this phone call short.

"Okay, come pick me up tomorrow. Here are directions to my apartment," Rob said and then gave directions to his apartment.

"I'll pick you up at nine o'clock," Tex said.

Now Rob had to make up a lie to his wife and think it up fast.

"Honey, guess what? I just got a catering job in Hawaii; I'm goin' tomorrow," Rob said.

Sheila was instantly suspicious.

"What do you mean a catering job in Hawaii? Don't they have waiters in Hawaii? What is going on here? You're lying to me! Are you involved in drugs?! Is that where that money came from? Nobody makes fifteen hundred dollars off of a one-night waitering job. You're lyin' to me! What's going on here?! Is it drugs? Is that what you're into? Honey, if that's what it is, you've got to get out. You're puttin' the baby and me in danger. These are real bad guys. They'll kill you if you cross them. Look, I'll get a job as a waitress. We can live on that. You can stay home with the baby until you make it in the business," Sheila said.

"Look, I got a waitering job in Hawaii, and I'm going to take it, and that's final," Rob said flatly.

"Oh, I know you're hiding something from me!" Sheila screamed.

Yet Rob was adamant. He was going to Hawaii. This was an extra thousand dollars for rent and groceries. He was not passing this up.

The next day Rob packed up in one of Sheila's suitcases. Then he headed out the door. He waited for Tex in front of the apartment. Tex drove up shortly in his Cadillac.

"Hop in, pretty boy," Tex bellowed.

"Look, don't call me pretty boy or the trip is off, and another thing, you said a thousand for the trip. I want my money now," Rob growled.

"Okay, okay, cool down," Tex said nervously.

He pulled out a wad of one hundred dollar bills and handed them to Rob.

"We're gonna have a good time in Hawaii. Have you ever been there?"

Rob said that he had not. Tex told him that he would like Hawaii. They were going to the big island of Oahu. Tex drove to the airport and parked in long-term parking. Then they boarded their flight-first class, Tex always flew first class-and they flew to Hawaii.

Rob was immediately taken with Hawaii-the cool, tropical climate, the beaches, the lush vegetation. Rob and Tex stayed at a five-star hotel on Waikiki Beach. By day, Rob took surfing lessons and worked on his tan. Rob and Tex made a study in contrasts. Rob was studly, handsome, and muscular, and Tex corpulent and flabby. Who would have guessed that they were a couple? At night, they attended a luau, where Rob danced with the women hula dancers. He was very popular with these hula dancers. Yet after the luaus, Rob would have to return to the hotel room and let Tex worship his body. This repulsed Rob, but a thousand dollars was a thousand dollars! Much as he was enjoying himself, Rob started to count the days. Tex loved to watch Rob step out of the shower and towel him-self off. Tex would put his arms around Rob's back while Rob shaved and brushed his teeth. Then it was back to the beach for more surfing. After a week, it was time to return to Los

Angeles. Rob was sorry to leave Hawaii but was not sad to leave Tex's cloying embrace.

Back in Los Angeles, Tex drove Rob to his apartment. Tex looked around and saw no one around.

"Give me a smacker on the lips," Tex demanded.

Rob was repulsed.

"Look, we're out in public," Rob protested.

"No one can see us," Tex interjected.

Tex leaned over and gave a big smoochy kiss on Rob's lips.

"Okay, you've had your kiss; goodbye," Rob growled.

"Let's get together this weekend," Tex said plaintively. "I'll pay you another thousand."

"Okay," Rob said.

"Then it's a date. I'll pick you up here at seven on Friday," Tex said, as he was looking forward to another date with Rob.

Rob walked up the stairs to his apartment building. He entered his apartment.

"Hi honey, I'm home," Rob said excitedly to his wife.

"And look what I've brought," Rob said while pulling out a wad of one thousand dollars.

"Oh, they do drug dealing in Hawaii too?" Sheila asked sarcastically.

Rob felt exasperated.

"Look, I told you. I got a catering job in Hawaii," Rob growled.

"Don't look at me and lie to me. This is drug money, isn't it?" Sheila asked accusatorially.

"Stop accusing me of drug dealing! I'm not involved in anything like that. Why can't you believe that I'm just getting catering jobs?" Rob asked plaintively.

"Because no one pays a thousand dollars for catering jobs in Hawaii. They have waiters in Hawaii. They don't need to fly them in. Rob, you're in trouble. All this money, all this flying around, you're into something dangerous. I'm scared. I want to help, but I can't until you tell me the truth. What's going on here? Where is this money coming from? It's drugs, isn't it? I just know it's drugs! Sheila said accusatorially.

Rob could not tell his wife he had spent the past week servicing an old man. He had to stick to his lie.

"Look, honey; it was a catering job. That's all, and look at the money I made! We're set for the next month!" Rob said excitedly.

"Oh, great, another month, and then what, another drug deal? Next time, you could get caught by the police! Then what? Do you know what could happen to your career? You'd never get cast in a TV series or a film with a drug conviction on your record!" Sheila screamed.

Rob had to calm Sheila down. He grabbed Sheila to calm her down, but she broke free and hit Rob on his chest.

"Don't try to put me off. I know this is drug money," Sheila screamed.

Rob screamed back.

"I told you this was a catering job, and I expect you to believe me when I tell you something," Rob said.

"Believe you when you tell me something!?! You lie and lie and lie, and you expect me to believe your lies? I'll never believe you when you lie!" Sheila screamed back.

"That's it! I've had it with you! I'"m leavin' 'til you cool down," Rob shouted and stormed out the door.

"Rob, don't you go walking out on me! You come back here!" Sheila shouted.

Yet it did no good. Rob continued to storm out. Sheila started to cry. She did not know what to do. She knew Rob was in trouble but could do nothing about it. She sat down in despair. What to do? Meanwhile, Rob had stormed out into the street. He wondered where the nearest bar was.

3

Chris finished opening up another lawsuit file. Chris worked for an insurance defense law firm as a file clerk. Among law firms, insurance defense law firms were at the bottom of the barrel. He earned about $24,000 a year. He was overworked and underpaid. It was Friday afternoon-a time Chris always liked. It meant he could escape this hell hole for two days. Any time away from here he looked forward to. He usually spent Friday, Saturday, and Sunday evenings in the bars. He loved to have a good time.

He overheard one of the lawyers talking to his legal secretary. "My doctor friend let me put on a white lab coat and walk into the examining room where a woman patient was in a hospital gown. Then the doctor let me watch while he examined the woman patient. She thought I was a doctor because I wore a white lab coat. I didn't tell you when and where this happened. So you can't go to the police about it. And with that, the lawyer went into his office.

These lawyers are so sick, Chris thought.

After working for this law firm for two years, Chris had a dim view of lawyers.

Another thing he disapproved of was a photo of a bare-breasted woman in the law firm files. This woman had burn scars on her breasts. To gather evidence, a woman secretary took photos of the woman's burn scars on her breasts. For the lawyers, these photos were almost like the office copy of Play-boy. At least once a day, some of the lawyers were ogling at the photos of this poor woman.

At five o'clock, Chris turned off his computer and left. He went to Roby's bar on Santa Monica Boulevard in West Hollywood every Friday. Chris could not afford to live in West Hollywood, even though it had rent control. Chris took the bus to Santa Monica and Vine Streets in Hollywood. At Vine, he transferred to the Santa Monica bus. It carried him into West Hollywood. He got off the Santa Monica bus in West Holly-wood and went to the ATM halfway down the block. He pulled out $40.

Then he went to Roby's bar. The bar was almost empty at this hour. There were two other people there. Friday nights were busy for Roby's. However, the evening crowd would not come in for another three hours. Until then, Chris slid onto a bar stool and ordered a vodka tonic. At six o'clock, the male go-go dancers came into the bar. The go-go dancers liked Chris. Not only was Chris attractive, but he was a good tipper too. Chris represented guaranteed money for the go-go dancers.

One of the go-go dancers, Jose, walked into the bar and climbed up on a small stage. Jose was a knockout. He was 5'6" and weighed 185 pounds of lean muscle. He had a very muscu-lar body that few people could resist. His face was almost per-fect. Jose was a very handsome man. Chris just went bonkers over him. Jose was only wearing a G-string and heavy black work boots. Jose smiled at Chris and started dancing. Chris waved hello to him and ordered another drink. It would take Chris two drinks before the alcohol loosened his inhibitions, and he went over to Jose and put a dollar bill in Jose's G-string. Jose liked Chris and was always glad to get the money, and then he gave Chris a light kiss on the cheek. Jose had power over Chris because Chris could not resist Jose, and Jose knew it and loved his power over Chris.

After three drinks, Chris decided that he was hungry. He was sloshed from the drinks. What restaurant would Chris go to? There were only expensive restaurants or pizza joints along this stretch of Santa Monica Boulevard. Chris then remembered Letters restaurant. Letters had a terrible reputation because of the gigolos who frequented the bar. However, the food there was good, and Chris wanted to treat himself tonight. He waved goodbye to Jose and left the bar. He walked down Santa Monica to Letters. He climbed the stairs to Letters and walked into the restaurant.

The first thing he noticed was how dark this place was. It was almost empty too. He squinted and looked around the restaurant. It was seven o'clock, and the dinner crowd had not arrived yet. A very handsome maitre'd in a black outfit walked up to him and asked Chris if he wanted a table. Chris said yes and was shown to a table. Along the wall, there were booths. Between the booths and the bar was a row of small tables. Chris was seated at one of these tables. The maitre'd gave Chris a menu.

"Our specialty today is prime rib. Your waiter will be here in a minute," the maitre'd said and walked away.

Just then, an equally handsome waiter in a black outfit walked up to Chris' table.

"Hello, I'm Randy; I'll be your waiter tonight. Would you care for a drink before ordering dinner?" Randy asked.

Chris already had three drinks, but the thought of another drink pleased him.

"Yes, I'd like a whiskey sour," Chris said.

"Straight up or on the rocks," Randy asked.

"Straight up," Chris answered.

"I'll be right back with your drink," Randy said, and he went to the bar to fetch Chris' drink.

Chris looked around the bar. It was mostly empty. He looked out the window to the traffic on Santa Monica Boulevard. Then he read the menu. Letters was an expensive restaurant, and Chris did not make all that much money. However, it was Friday, and Chris wanted to splurge. Randy returned with Chris' drink.

"Are you ready to order yet?" Randy asked.

"Yes, I'll have the prime rib," Chris said.

"Baked potato or mashed potato?" Randy asked.

"Baked potato, please," Chris answered.

"What kind of salad dressing do you want? Randy asked.

"Oh, blue cheese," Chris answered.

"All right then, I'll be back shortly with your dinner," Randy said, turning and walking to the kitchen. There were not many people in here to people watch, which was one of Chris' favorite hobbies. He had had four drinks by now, and they were taking their effect on him. He felt sloshed. After a while, his order arrived. Chris dug in. Notorious bar or no, this restaurant sure had good food, Chris thought. Some people came over simply for the food. Chris asked his waiter for a glass of white Zinfandel with his dinner. Chris thought that the food would keep him sober. He did not realize that food would not keep him sober. It did not take him long to wolf down his dinner. He ordered a piece of strawberry cheesecake and a cup of coffee for dessert. He ate the dessert with relish and gulped down his coffee. When the check arrived, he blanched. The check was for $50. And this dinner was just one person! Imagine what the check would be like for two people, Chris thought. Chris was glad that he had his credit card with him. He had just about enough available credit on his credit card to charge this dinner.

He whipped out his credit card, paid for the dinner, and gave a 20% tip to his waiter. He had another cup of coffee.

Then he decided to go to the bar and hang out for a little while. It was eight o'clock, and the bar was beginning to fill up. Watching the front door from the bar was a study in contrasts. Fat, pot-bellied, and bald men were walking in. So were some very handsome young men. Chris ogled these handsome young men. He ordered his fifth drink of the night, another whiskey sour. He continued to look at these very handsome men. He would love to get together with one of these guys, but he did not have enough money. At $24,000 a year, he had little disposable income. He looked and longed after the handsome young men. After his fifth drink, he had a sixth drink. He was not keeping count of his drinks and did not realize that he had drunk six drinks. One of the handsome young men there was named Tim. Tim saw Chris and wondered if Chris had enough money to pay for him tonight. Chris certainly looked better than these old trolls at the bar. Tim decided to talk to Chris. Tim walked up to Chris.

"Hello, I'm Tim, and you are?" Tim asked.

Chris was taken by surprise by Tim.

"I'm Chris... Chris," Chris answered.

"Well, it's nice to see you, Chris. We don't get many cute guys like you here." Tim said.

"Thanks...thank you," Chris said.

"What are you drinking?" Tim asked.

"A whiskey sour," Chris answered.

"I've never had a whiskey sour before. What do they taste like?" Tim asked.

Tim was looking to see if Chris was generous. If Chris were generous, Tim would have his "appointment" for the night.

"They taste very sour, but I like that," Chris answered.

"Would you like one?" Chris asked.

Bingo, Tim told himself. This kid's got enough money for me tonight, he thought.

"Sure, I'd like a drink," Tim said.

Chris turned to the bartender and ordered Tim a whiskey sour. They clinked their glasses together and said, "Cheers." They talked animatedly with each other for an hour. After another round of drinks-this was Chris' seventh drink. Tim got down to business.

"For five hundred dollars, you can come home with me tonight," Tim said.

This was the second time that Chris was taken by surprise by Tim. Five hundred dollars!?! I don't have that kind of money, Chris thought.

"Look, I don't have that kind of money," Chris said.

"Well, how much do you have? Look, this is Letters. You know the score. How much money do you have?" Tim answered sarcastically.

Chris would love to get together with Tim. Tim was one of the most handsome men here. Yet he could not afford $500 to pay Tim. Chris had rent, groceries, and credit cards to pay. He could not afford $500. Chris thought about how much he could spare and still pay his monthly bills. He guessed that he could spare $300.

"Well, I guess I could pay three hundred," Chris said hesitantly.

"Okay, three hundred it is. Finish your drink and let's get goin,'" Tim said.

Chris gulped down his seventh drink, and together with Tim, they left Letters. Chris and Tim walked up to a bank ATM. This was not Chris' bank, but Chris used it for convenience's sake. Chris put in his ATM card. He then pulled $300 out of the ATM. He handed the money over to Tim. Tim grabbed the money and started running off. When he had run half a block away, he turned to Chris, waved at him, and then turned and ran away. Chris was heartbroken. He could not afford $300, and now he had been robbed. Someday that guy is gonna hustle the wrong guy, Chris thought. He decided to go back to Letters and drink away his sorrows with an eighth drink.

At Letters, he stood at the bar, dejected about what had happened. He nursed his eighth drink. After about an hour, Chris saw the most handsome man he had ever seen walk into the bar. It was Rob. Rob was here again, looking for some easy money. He had managed to pay his rent and buy groceries, but in another month, he would need to pay rent and buy groceries again. Letters was a quick and easy way to make money. Rob scanned the bar. The usual old and dejected old men were there. Only a couple of gigolos were there. Yet, it's a little early for the hustlers to get here. Rob thought this place would be crawling with hustlers in a few hours. At the bar sat Chris, alone and dejected. He's new-what a cute little Twinkie. I hope he has some money to spend tonight, Rob thought. Rob saddled up to the bar next to Chris.

"Hello, I'm Rob; who are you?" Rob asked.

Chris was taken by surprise by this question. Chris could not believe his luck. Rob was the most handsome man in the bar, and he was talking to Chris! Chris' mood immediately improved.

Chris, my name is Chris," Chris answered.

Despite being burned by one young gigolo tonight, Chris decided to take another chance.

"Can I buy you a drink?" Chris asked plaintively.

Oh great, this guy's not a hustler. Rob thought he was the cutest little Twinkie in the bar, and I could have him all to him-self tonight, in addition to making some more easy money.

"A Scotch and soda," Rob answered.

Chris ordered a Scotch and soda for Rob. He did not order himself another drink. Even though he had eight drinks by now, he had not kept track but knew he was drinking too much. Chris paid for the drink and handed it to Rob. Rob swallowed two gulps of his drink. Then he slowed down. Much as he loved Scotch and soda, he did not want to get drunk tonight. Chris continued to nurse his eighth drink. Rob finished his first drink, and then Chris offered him another one.

Chris really could not afford to keep buying rounds of drinks, but Chris was drunk and horny by now. He was not thinking about money and affordability now. At the end of the month, he would receive his credit card bill and be stunned by how much he had spent tonight. Yet tonight, he wanted to get alone with Rob. He wondered where he would get the money.

After Rob's second drink, Rob decided to move in for the kill.

"Would you like to go off someplace private tonight?" Rob asked.

"What will it cost me?" Chris asked nervously.

Rob usually charged $1,000, but he would give a discount for this cute little Twinkie. He decided on $500.

"Five hundred dollars," Rob answered.

Chris was taken aback by surprise by this. He did not have $500.

"Sorry, I don't have that much," Chris answered disappointedly.

Rob was angry. What was he doing at Letters if he could not afford the hustlers here? Rob thought.

"Well, what are you doing at Letters?" Rob asked.

"I don't know," Chris answered sheepishly.

"See you around," Rob said and walked away.

Chris was crestfallen for the second time this night. First, the other guy, now Rob, Chris thought. How could the evening get any worse?" Chris thought to himself.

Rob went to the other end of the bar and looked at the old men sitting dejectedly at the bar. He did not want to go anywhere with these trolls tonight. He had been hoping that Chris would be able to afford him tonight.

Yet then, Chris had an idea. He had a credit card. He would take a cash advance on his credit card. That way, he would be able to afford Rob at $500. He walked up to Rob.

"Listen, I can pay you five hundred," Chris said nervously.

"Great, let's get out of here," Rob said, his mood improving by this turn of events. Now, he would not have to go anywhere with these trolls. He had a cute little Twinkie paying him easy money for sex. Life was looking good, Rob thought.

Rob swallowed the remnants of his Scotch and soda, and he and Chris walked out of Letters. They walked to the nearest bank ATM. Chris put his credit card in the slot and used his password to withdraw $500 from the ATM. Five hundred dollars came out in $20 bills. Chris hesitated to hand the money to Rob, especially after Tim robbed him. Chris put the money in his pocket, and Rob and Chris walked to the nearest hotel. Chris would also put that on the credit card too. This was turning into a costly evening, and Chris could barely afford it.

They walked into the hotel and up to the front desk.

"I need a room for the night," Chris told the desk clerk.

"Single occupancy or double occupancy?" the desk clerk asked.

"Double occupancy," Chris answered.

"Do you have any luggage?" the desk clerk asked.

Chris was embarrassed by this. He did not have any luggage, and he did not know what to say. So he made up a lie.

"My luggage was lost at the airport," Chris lied.

"Oh, I'm sorry," the desk clerk said.

"How much is the room?" Chris asked nervously

"Five hundred dollars," the desk clerk answered.

Chris pulled his credit card out and paid the fee. He knew he would regret this when he received his credit card bill at the end of the month.

With that, the desk clerk handed Chris a plastic card that was a room key for room number 222. Chris and Rob went to the elevator and went up to room 222.

"Did you get a load of that?" the desk clerk asked the other desk clerk.

"Maybe we should charge them by the hour," the other desk clerk said. They both laughed at that.

Chris fumbled with the card key. Rob stepped in and used the card key to open the door. When the door opened, Rob held the door open for Chris to enter the room. Then Rob walked into the room and shut the door.

Chris was as nervous as he could be. He did not want to be rolled again tonight. Yet, he would love to have a chance to be alone with Rob. Rob sensed Chris' nervousness.

"It's all right; I'm not going to hurt you or cheat you. You're cute. I want you. You can service me all you want," Rob said.

Chris hesitantly pulled out the $500 and gave it to Rob. Rob quickly counted it and put it in his pants pocket. Then Rob pulled off his shirt. Chris was dazzled by Rob's muscular torso. Rob was the most beautiful man Chris had ever seen. Chris never thought he would have a chance with a guy as handsome as Rob. Chris melted in Rob's arms.

4

The following Friday, Chris decided to go back to Letters. Hopefully, he would find Rob there. Despite the high cost of the evening, it had been the most exotic and erotic night of Chris' life. Chris was getting into debt by going back to Letters. However, he was captivated by Rob, and debt or no debt; he was determined to get together with Rob again. Chris had dinner at Letters. The food was good at Letters. After dinner, he found a place at the bar and waited for Rob to arrive.

Rob arrived about an hour later. Son, the county doesn't pay us to send you out on dates, Rob heard one of his voices say. After his rendezvous with Chris, Rob had enough to pay the rent. That still left groceries to pay for, so Rob was back at Letters. He needed money for groceries. Rob was also hoping that Chris would be there. Chris was a lot more fun than these old geysers, and Chris paid $500 to boot. Two rendezvous with Chris, Rob would have his rent, grocery money, and a little extra money to take his wife out for an evening again. Rob walked into Letters and scanned the crowd for Chris. Chris was at the far end of the bar waiting for Rob. Rob walked up to Chris and held out his arms for a hug.

"Hello, amigo. Good to see you again," Rob said.

"Good to see you too. Can I buy you a drink?" Chris asked.

"Sure thing, a Scotch and soda," Rob answered.

Chris had opened a tab, and the bartender put the drink on Chris' tab.

"Cheers," Rob said as he and Chris clinked their glasses together.

Chris decided to strike up a conversation with Rob.

"What did you do today?" Chris asked.

"Not much; I got up late. I played with my baby for most of the afternoon," Rob said.

Chris was immediately shocked. A baby? A baby! Does he have a baby?

"You have a baby? Chris asked in astonishment.

"Yes, I do. She's only a few months old, and she's adorable. Here I have a picture of her," Rob said as he pulled a photo out of his wallet and showed it to Chris.

"Isn't she adorable?" Rob asked.

"Sure, yeah, she's adorable," Chris answered in shock.

Chris did not want to have sex with a married man for any reason. This was the worst possible news that he could have. Chris was not sure that he could engage in sex with a married man- a married man with a baby to boot. Chris excused himself and went to the restroom. He was not sure that he could see Rob again. He splashed water on his face. Then he looked into the mirror and wondered what to do. He did not want to get involved with a married man. Yet Rob was the most handsome man he had ever met. He could not resist Rob. He decided that he would think about this later. As it was, he wanted Rob desperately, and marriage or no marriage, Chris could not resist Rob. He walked out of the restroom. Back in the bar, Chris saw an old man talking to Rob. Chris decided to stay around for a few moments.

When Chris entered the restroom, an old man at the bar walked up to Rob.

"Hello, my dear boy, it's good to see you. I haven't seen you in here much before now. I'm glad to see you. We need some new blood in here. And may I say that you're the most handsome man here," the old man said.

Rob was surprised by such a bold action by this old man. Rob had Chris, and he wanted to avoid any old geysers tonight.

"I'm throwing a birthday party for a friend of mine. We're going to throw a raffle. I want you to be the "prize" for the raffle."

This old man immediately repulsed Rob.

'I'll pay you two thousand dollars for the evening," the old man said.

Two thousand dollars?! Rob gasped. That's a lot of money. That would pay four months' rent or buy two months' worth of groceries. I can't afford to pass this up, Rob thought. The old man had made an offer that Rob could not refuse.

"Okay, I'll do it, but I'm telling you right now. I'm not about to be the "prize" at a raffle. And I'll only do it with one guy. You choose among yourselves who that winner is going to be. And when is this party going on? And another thing, what's your name?"

The old man was startled by this outburst from Rob.

"Steve, my name is Steve. I guess we should have exchanged names and pleasantries first," Steve said.

"Okay, and another thing. I get paid in advance. If I go to this thing, and there's no money. I'm walkin' out," Rob said with a stern tone to his voice.

Steve thought that these conditions were onerous. However, Rob was the most handsome man in the room, and he could set his price.

"Deal, it's a deal, dear boy," Steve said and held out his hand to shake hands on the deal.

"Deal," Rob said.

"Say, when is this party?" Rob asked.

"Why it's tomorrow night, dear boy. I live up in the hills-the Swish Alps as they're called. How about I pick you up here tomorrow night, and we'll go to my place for the party?" Steve asked.

"Sounds good to me," Rob said.

"Maybe you'd like to come up there with me tonight, dear boy?" Steve asked.

Rob looked around the bar and saw Chris just a few feet away. He would prefer to spend this night with Chris. Even at $500 a night, Rob could still profit from Chris. He motioned for Chris to come over.

"Not tonight, guy. I'm already taken for tonight," Rob said to Steve.

"Well, then tomorrow night it is, dear boy. I'll see you here at six o'clock tomorrow evening. Don't do what I wouldn't do," Steve said, and with that, he returned to his friends at one of the restaurant's booths. Steve's friends asked Steve how well things had gone with Rob. Steve told his friends that Rob's name was Rob.

"I've got him for tomorrow night at the raffle party I'm throwing, Be sure to bring one hundred dollar bills. A man who looks as good as Rob can command hundreds or even thousands of dollars." Steve said.

"Well, how much are you paying him?" one of the old men asked.

"Two thousand dollars and I'm sure he's worth every cent of it," Steve said.

"Two thousand dollars!?! That's outrageous. That's highway robbery," the old man said.

"These boys go where the money is. You have to pay them, or they won't be comin' around. I'm prepared to pay any price in order to get these boys or young men, I should say," Steve said.

Looking at the bar, Steve and his friends saw Rob leave with Chris.

"Who's he leaving with?" the old man said.

"I don't know. I've never seen him before," Steve said.

"Well, the boy he's leaving with certainly is cute. Say, maybe we could get those two to put on a show for us. A little show of man-to-man action. Wouldn't that be wonderful?" the old man gushed.

"Let's not be greedy. Tomorrow night, Rob will be ours, and one lucky raffle winner will win Rob, " Steve said.

Rob walked to the hotel with Chris. Rob was feeling pretty good. Five hundred dollars tonight, two thousand dollars tomorrow night. Life is good, Rob thought. He had thought that he would do this only once, but the allure of the money was too much. He was keeping this a secret. Rob thought this was easy money; no one would ever know about it.

Promptly at six, Rob walked into Letters. He had told his wife that he was going to a catering job again. She did not believe his stories about a caterer who paid in cash. Yet there was nothing she could do about it. The old man named Steve was already waiting at the bar. Rob walked up to him.

"Well, hello, dear boy. How nice to see you. And you're on time too. Punctuality is very important," Steve said.

"Before this goes any further, I want my money, and I want it now," Rob demanded

"Oh, dear boy. You can't expect me to pay you here in this bar with all these people watching. I'll pay you once we get in the car. This is how I'll pay you. I'll pay you a thousand dollars before the party, and I'll pay you another thousand dollars at the end of the party. Let's leave now," Steve said.

Steve had become afraid that Rob would take the money and run. This was Steve's insurance policy that Rob would not take the money and run. Rob did not like this turn of events. Yet he was powerless to stop it. Rob would not have taken the money and run, but Steve did not know. They went to the parking garage and got into Steve's Mercedes Benz. Steve whipped out a stack of ten $100 bills and handed it to Rob.

"You don't have to worry with me, dear boy. I'll pay you what we agreed on. It's just that I'll pay you over two payments. But I will pay you," Steve said.

Rob was surprised by the two payment plans. However, there was nothing he could do about it.

Steve and Rob drove to Steve's house in Bel Air. I'm gettin' to know this area like the back of my hand, Rob thought. Son, the county doesn't pay us to send you out on dates, Rob's voice said. They drove to Steve's house, high in the hills. Upon reaching the house, Steve and Rob walked in. There were six guys with drinks sitting around in the living room.

"Look at this pulchritudinous prize," Steve said to the men.

The men pulled out their cell phone cameras and started taking pictures of Rob. Rob was angry now. He grabbed Steve's lapels and pushed Steve against the wall.

"I told you not to call me a prize," Rob said angrily. Then he turned to the group of assorted old men.

"Turn those cameras off, or I'm leavin'," Rob growled at them.

Rob did not want any photos taken during this evening. If those photos got on the Internet, there would be no deleting those photos, and those photos would follow him around for the rest of his life.

With that, the old men put their cell phones down.

Then Rob turned back to Steve.

"Anything you want. Anything at all, dear boy," Steve said fearfully.

"And stop calling me dear boy. I'm not a boy. I'm a man," Rob spit these words out to Steve. "Now, where is some privacy around here?" Rob demanded.

"Upstairs... there are some bedrooms upstairs. You can go into any one of them. There's complete privacy there," Steve answered nervously. Steve was scared that Rob would turn violent.

"Good, I'm going to go up there, and you can send one, just one, person up there to service me," Rob growled. "And you're not going to cheat me out of my money, either," Rob continued as he let go of Steve.

Sure thing, dear boy. Anything you say. Would you like a drink first?" Steve asked.

"I thought I told you not to call me dear boy," Rob lashed out.

Steve thought getting some alcohol into Rob would calm Rob down. However, alcohol made some people violent, and Rob was one of these people. Steve did not know what he would do if Rob turned violent. It was worth it to give Rob his second one thousand dollars and send him on his way. Steve hurriedly fixed Rob a drink, a Scotch, and soda, Rob's favorite drink. Rob gulped his drink down in a few gulps. Then Rob announced that he was going upstairs and that only one person could come into the bedroom to service Rob. With that, Rob went upstairs. He entered the bedroom to his right.

Meanwhile, downstairs, the old men had been given small pieces of paper with a number on them.

"Who has five hundred?" Steve asked.

One of the old men squealed with delight. He had the winning raffle ticket. Rob was going to be his tonight. This old man's name was Ron. He was a casting director. He could have any aspiring actor he wanted. Yet Rob was, by far, the most handsome man he had ever seen.

"Step right upstairs to claim your prize," Steve announced.

Every one of the old men watched enviously as Ron walked up to his rendezvous with Rob. In the bedroom, Rob had taken his shirt off. Ron walked into the room.

"You certainly are the most handsome man I've ever seen," Ron said.

"Can I see you with your clothes off?" Ron inquired.

With that, Rob pulled off his pants and did a few muscle poses for Ron. Ron walked up to Rob and hugged Rob. He melted in Rob's arms.

Afterward, Ron said: "I could get you some work. Let's get together for dinner tomorrow to discuss your career. I would love to get together with you tomorrow night. I'll be happy to pay your fee. By the way, what do you charge? Ron said

Rob decided to keep his price at $2,000 and told Ron so.

After this little escapade, Ron left. Rob put his clothes on and walked to the staircase. He walked up to the front of the stairs. He called for Steve. Rob wanted to be paid the remainder of what was due to him. Steve came up the staircase.

"I want my money, and I want it now," Rob growled.

"Yes, of course," Steve said. Steve whipped out a bundle of hundred-dollar bills. He took out $1,000 in hundred-dollar bills and handed them to Rob. Rob quickly counted the hundred dollar bills and put them in his pocket.

"Okay, can you call me a cab?" Rob asked.

"Sure, thing, dear boy...Oh, I'm sorry. I can call you a cab," Steve said.

Rob and Steve walked down the stairs to the living room. The ugly old men whipped out their cameras again and started taking photos. Rob became angry. He did not want any photos of this night to get on the Internet, even if he was entirely dressed-the fewer photos of him, the better.

"I told you old geysers, no photos," Rob yelled.

Rob approached one of the old men, grabbed his camera, and threw it against the wall.

"When I tell you no cameras, I mean no cameras," Rob yelled.

Rob could have a nasty temper sometimes. The thought of these photos getting on the Internet worried him. The photos of him showed him fully dressed. However, he again thought the fewer photos of him, the better. The old men were frightened by this violent outburst. They put their cameras away.

Rob and Steve walked to the front door. One of the old men wanted to have a chance with Rob. This old man's name was George. George had been panting after Rob all evening. He was heartbroken that he had not won the raffle. George decided to take a chance. When Steve said he would call for a cab, George saw his opportunity to be with Rob and stepped in immediately.

"Oh, you don't need a cab. I can drive you home," George said.

Rob and Steve looked at each other, and then Rob said okay.

Before he left, though, Steve wanted to make another "date" with Rob.

"How about next week? We do another party like tonight. I'll pay you two thousand again, of course," Steve said.

Rob was eager to come back. He had just cleared $2,000. All for letting these old geysers service him. It was the easiest $2,000 he had ever made. Rob and Steve exchanged phone numbers.

"See you next week. Pick me up at Letters at six next Friday, and we've got a date," Rob said.

George said goodnight to Steve, putting his hand on Rob's shoulders.

"Come along, my dear. Times' a wastin'," George said.

George was tinkled pink that Rob was going home with him. George went in for the kill.

"Why don't we stop by my place for a nightcap?" George asked.

Rob was tired, and he wanted to go home.

"I'm really tired right now," Rob answered.

"I'll pay you as much as Steve just did," George said breathlessly.

"You'll pay me two thousand dollars?" Rob asked.

George was surprised. He thought that Steve had paid Rob $1,000. George only had about $1,000 on him.

"Uh, no...well, no. I only have a thousand dollars on me," George said.

Rob thought about it for a moment. An extra one thousand dollars was all right after all. He decided to agree to this.

"Okay, for a thousand dollars, I'll do it, but just remember. The next time, it's two thousand," Rob said.

Rob was becoming accustomed to charging large sums of money from lonely and horny old men. He was starting to build up a clientele.

George was overjoyed. He would love to have Rob all to himself tonight. He readily agreed to pay two thousand next time.

George pulled up to the driveway at his condominium building. The building was along the Golden Mile of condominium towers along Wilshire Boulevard. These condominiums cost at least $1 million. One penthouse condominium had sold for $11 million. Rob was starting to hobnob with some very wealthy people. He walked through the lobby with George, and suddenly, Rob felt poor-considering the difference between this luxury tower and his shabby apartment building in Hollywood. They went up to George's condominium. It was tastefully furnished. The furniture cost probably in the thousands. George,

however, could easily afford that. He was a high-powered part-
ner at one of the biggest law firms in the city, indeed in
the country. He could easily afford costly furniture and Rob's
asking price of $1,000.

"Would you like a drink?" George asked.

"Yes, I would," Rob answered.

"What'll it be?" George asked.

"A Scotch and soda," Rob answered.

George poured the drinks with his shaking hands. He was
very nervous about having Rob in his condominium. Rob had
unleashed his anger at the old men back at the party. George
did not want Rob to show his temper here, not now, not
tonight. He handed Rob the drink. When the drinks were finished, George decided to make his move.

"How about we get out of these clothes and have a wrestling
match," George asked.

Rob could barely stand the thought of a wrestling match
with this old geyser. However, it cost $1,000, and Rob would
only stay here for an hour.

"Sure thing, old man," Rob answered.

They both undressed, and George stepped up to Rob. George
hugged Rob and melted into Rob's arms.

Afterward, Rob got dressed and started to leave. George
called after him.

"Look, let's do this again. How 'bout next Friday?" George
asked.

"Okay, I'll come here this Friday at six o'clock. Just remember, next Friday, it's two thousand dollars, or I walk," Rob
answered.

"Okay," George said.

And with that, Rob left. He had cleared $3,500 in just one
weekend. Please consider how much he could expect to earn
for another weekend. He also wondered about charging more

money. He saw that he could clear $2,000 from Steve. From now on, I'll charge these old geysers two thousand dollars a pop. He had the doorman call him a cab. A month ago, he did not have the money for the rent. Now he was taking cabs with $3,500 in his pocket. This money would give him the freedom to pursue his acting career. As they say, some of the old geysers at that party were in the business. Maybe they could get him some acting jobs? Maybe his dreams of becoming an actor were near fulfillment. No one would know about this prostituting himself. That would remain a big secret.

However, one of the old men named John, who had taken Rob's photo, was going to show Rob's photo to his friend. This friend would play a pivotal role in Rob's life. Rob did not know it yet.

Rob went to Letters again. When he arrived at Letters, he stopped. Parked alongside the curb were a police van and two police cars.

"What's goin' on here?" he asked himself.

Meanwhile, upstairs in Letters, five plainclothes police officers from the Los Angeles County Sheriff's Department vice squad had entered the cocktail lounge. They walked across the length of the cocktail lounge. At a signal, all the vice squad officers pulled out their badges, and one officer yelled:

"This is the vice squad, and this is a raid! Everyone near the bar is under arrest!"

The bar's young men, including Bob and Tom-the, wanna-be actors, would be charged with prostitution. The older men would be charged with solicitation. Rob had narrowly missed out on being caught up in a vice raid. The gigolos and old men were lined up near the door. The people in the dining section of the restaurant were not arrested. The owner of the restaurant was apoplectic. Not only was this bad publicity, but it could also lead to the revocation of his liquor license. That would shut down his business. He did not know what to do.

The people by the bar were lined up by the door and placed in plastic handcuffs. Each one was read his Miranda rights. Then each one was marched by two officers and placed in the police van, which was the current term for the paddy wagon. Bob and Tom bitterly realized that their dreams of becoming movie stars were abruptly over. What did I do to deserve this? I haven't hurt anybody. This is a victimless crime. I thought the police were supposed to leave us alone here! Now, what am I going to do? They were then transported to the West Hollywood Sheriff's Station. There they were photographed, fingerprinted, and booked. They were allowed one phone call. On Monday morning, they were transported by bus to the downtown criminal courts building, where they were arraigned. Everyone pleaded not guilty, and they were released on their own recognizance. They did not need to post bail. However, now every one of them would need to hire lawyers. Those who could not afford lawyers would be given an overworked public defender.

For the older professional men, this was a problem, but not an insurmountable one. They could afford the best lawyers and could plead their solicitation charges down to misdemeanors.

Who were screwed were the gigolos. They could not afford the best legal talent. They would have to rely on public defenders. Public defenders were always overworked and overburdened. They did not have time to give as much individual attention as each client deserved. With a vice squad officer testifying against each gigolo, each gigolo would be convicted of prostitution. This felony conviction would follow the gigolo for the rest of his life. He would never work for the federal government, a bank, or a department store because they all used the same blacklist. In California, someone convicted of prostitution could not get a real estate license. So working as a real estate agent was out of the question too! Indeed, their chances of making it as an actor were out of the question too! Any dreams of stardom for the gigolos were now dashed forever!

Rob watched as the gigolos and the old men were loaded into the paddy wagon. He was shaken. Another few minutes, and that would have been him in the paddy wagon! His life would have been destroyed! He would never have been cast in a TV series or a film with a prostitution conviction on his record! He might have had to do time in jail or prison for this! He would have to rely on Tex and his regulars from now on. He hoped that would be enough to carry him over. He did not dare to advertise in gay magazines or on the Internet. The vice squad hunted down the gigolos there too. Why can't they leave us alone? We're not hurting anyone. Why can't they go after real crime? Rob thought.

He called his "appointment" for the night and arranged to be picked up at a different location. He would have to be much more careful from now on. He would only take on clients whom Tex and his others trusted clients.

5

Richard Jordon was one of the most powerful men in Hollywood. He had singlehandedly brought back the movie musical as the most profitable venture in the entertainment industry. His name was associated with the finest in family entertainment. He had a net worth of a billion dollars. However, Richard Jordan had dark secrets-namely teenage prostitution and sadomasochism. He practiced his sadomasochism on teenage male prostitutes and aspiring actors, who had been sent over to him by his friend John. If it ever got out publicly that he was an aficionado of teenage prostitution and sadomasochism, it would ruin his career. That was one of the reasons that he sought out male prostitutes and aspiring actors. The police would never do anything to Richard Jordan because of the accusations of male prostitutes and aspiring actors. Richard had too much power to be threatened by the police.

Richard Jordan was viciously violent to these teenage male prostitutes and aspiring actors. What he liked to do was to offer them a drink. He would put powdered chloral hydrate and powdered Nembutal in their drinks. This was the same combination that had killed Marilyn Monroe. Richard had one of his bodyguards take the hapless unconscious young man down to the basement when he passed out. Richard had turned his basement into a dungeon. The young man was laid on a bench and stripped.

Then Richard pulled a leather harness over his victim and handcuffed him to the wall. With the teenage male prostitute and aspiring actor harnessed and handcuffed, Richard turned on the video camcorder. Then he videotaped it as he sodomized the young man. Richard had quite a little collection of DVDs of raped male prostitutes. He kept dungeons in his Bel Air mansion, high in the foothills, and at his house in the Malibu colony. Richard loved to watch the videos of the raped young men while eating popcorn. It was very titillating for him. When the teenage male prostitutes and aspiring actors awoke, they found that they were harnessed and handcuffed. They invariably started screaming to be untied. Richard sent his bodyguard down into the dungeon to undo the poor wretched young man and kick him out the door-all without paying the prostitute a penny. Richard was cheap and greedy, and he loved to get sex for free from these prostitutes. Indeed, he bragged about it.

Richard had done this about a dozen times. However, the word was getting out on the prostitutes' hotline. Word spread quickly about Richard Jordan's kinky and violent activities. As a result, Richard had a hard time finding "new meat," which is how he referred to male prostitutes. By now, he was lucky that there were call boys who would have him.

However, word had not reached Rob about Richard. Rob was not yet on the prostitutes' hotline. One of the men at Steve's party, John, had taken a photo of Rob. John was a friend of Richard Jordan, and John helped Richard Jordan find "new meat" The day after the party at Steve's house, John showed Richard Jordan the photo of Rob. Richard was immediately taken with Rob's stunning handsomeness. Richard would love to tie Rob up and sodomize him.

"Get him for me," Richard ordered.

John said that he did not get Rob's phone number last night. It would take a little while to get that information. Richard ordered him to get Rob's phone number.

"You have twenty-four hours to get that guy's phone number," Richard ordered.

John said that he would do his best.

"I didn't say to do your best. I told you to get his phone number for me," Richard ordered again.

John said that he would get him the phone number. John really could not stand Richard Jordan; nobody could. However, Richard Jordan had power and money, and Jordan might give John some producing work for Jordan's next film project. A producing mention on a Richard Jordan film would open doors in the entertainment business for John. John was willing to act like a pimp for Richard Jordan to get this. John left Richard's mansion and called Steve, who had thrown the party with Rob last night.

"Steve, remember that guy at your party last night? Well, guess what? Richard Jordan wants to meet this guy. Give me his phone number so I can arrange a meeting," John said.

Steve was surprised by this phone call. He was in a quandary. Steve had heard all the rumors about Richard Jordan involving teenage prostitutes and sadomasochism. He was hesitant to give out Rob's phone number. On the other hand, if he did not give the phone number to Richard Jordan, then Richard Jordan could get Steve kicked out of the entertainment business, pronto. He decided to give out the phone number. John was pleased with the phone number. John thanked Steve profusely and offered to have lunch next week. This nonplused Steve. Steve was worried. He was curious whether Rob had heard all the rumors about Richard Jordan. Steve thought about warning Rob, but then he decided not to.

John telephoned Rob and introduced himself. He told Rob that Richard Jordan would love to meet him. Rob was surprised and overjoyed with this information. Rob was aware of Richard Jordan's fame. This guy can get me some jobs, Rob thought. Rob also decided to raise his "fee." Richard Jordan could quickly pay him $3,000, Rob thought. John told Rob that he would take Rob to Richard Jordan's place. They agreed to meet at a spot near Letters tomorrow night, and John would drive them up to Richard Jordan's Bel Air mansion. Rob was almost overjoyed. Richard Jordan, Richard Jordan, Rob thought. How lucky could he get? Yet, Rob also had a foreboding feeling too. He could not put it out of his mind, however. He decided to stop worrying. What could happen, he wondered?

The next night near Letters, Rob met up with John, Richard Jordan's pimp. John recognized Rob, but Rob did not remember John. Rob got into John's Mercedes Benz. Then they went to Richard Jordan's mansion in Bel Air. They both walked up to the front door. John opened the door and called in.

"Richard, oh, Richard, the young man is here," John said.

"Send him on in!" Richard ordered.

John stepped aside and motioned for Rob to enter the darkened house.

Darkness was all that Rob could see. This situation immediately took him aback. His feeling of foreboding had returned. Yet he stepped into the darkened house. He tried to make someone out, but it was too dark.

"Welcome to my lair," Richard Jordan said.

"Where are the lights? What's with this darkness? Turn the lights on!" Rob said.

"I'll turn them on when I feel like it," Richard Jordan growled.

"Look, you turn some lights on, or I'm leavin'," Rob said.

Richard did not want to miss out on a chance with Rob. He did not know how far he could push Rob. So he decided to turn on the lights. With one flick of the wrist, all the lights came on. Richard was standing in the middle of the living room. He looked at Rob with lust and awe. Rob was the most handsome man he had ever seen, and Richard was used to seeing pulchritudinous young men as film directors.

"Be still, my heart," Richard said as he approached Rob.

Richard put his hand on Rob's chest and started massaging Rob's chest. This immediately repulsed Rob. He pushed Richard away. Rob let old men service him and nothing more. He was not going to be pawed at by this old geyser.

"Look, no touching. I want my money, and I want it now," Rob ordered.

"You little punk! Do you know who I am? I'm Richard Jordan. I'm the most critical player in town. I can make or break you. Do you understand? When I want to touch you, I'll touch you, and you'll let me. Comprenez vous? Richard growled.

That was the truth. Richard could make or break Rob. If Rob wanted to get into "the business," he would have to kiss up to Richard Jordan. The thought of this appalled Rob, but he could do nothing about it.

"I want my money now," Rob growled back.

"I'll pay you when I'm good and ready to," Richard growled back.

"Now stand there. I want to take a picture of you," Richard said.

Photographs made Rob nervous. There was no telling where they might wind up on the Internet. However, Rob was fully dressed, and a photo of him fully clothed on the Internet would not hurt Rob. Richard told Rob to strip. Rob was surprised by this. No way Rob was going to undress on camera. That would hit the Internet and ruin any chance Rob might have for a career.

"Forget it. I want my money, and I want it now," Rob shouted.

"I told you I'd pay you when I felt like it and not a second more," Richard shouted.

So Rob decided to wait for his money. He did not like this. This situation was becoming stranger by the minute. Richard had much power, and Rob could not afford to get on Richard's wrong side. However, he stopped when Richard told Rob to take off his shirt.

Richard, however, wanted to calm Rob down. If Rob was not calmed down, he might bolt, and there went the evening's fun.

"I'll fix you a drink. What are ya drinkin' " Richard asked.

"A Scotch and soda," Rob answered.

Richard fixed the drink. The powered date rape drug was only inches away from Richard's hand. However, Richard did not want Rob to pass out yet. Richard had plans for the evening. Richard was going to a leather bar. Tonight was a slave boy's auction, and Richard did not want to miss it. Richard planned on "buying" one of these "slave boys" and returning him to his house. There he would slip date rape drugs into the boy's and Rob's drinks. Then he would have his bodyguard take them down to the basement. Then he would sodomize Rob and the "slave boy" and film the whole thing. Richard was looking forward eagerly to tonight. Richard and Rob got into Richard's Mercedes Benz and drove to Hollywood.

"Where are we goin'" Rob asked.

"I'm not payin' you to talk," Richard growled back.

The bar was in the seedy section of Hollywood, and Richard needed help finding a place to park. Once the car was parked, they walked to the leather bar. The bar was a little hole in the wall. It could pass as a warehouse or a garage. They walked into the bar. At the front door was a small desk where the bar patrons had to pay a cover charge. The bar's owner liked "slave boy night" because he brought in much money in cover charges. This was in addition to what he charged for watered-down drinks. The cover charge was $20. Richard told Rob that Richard did not have any cash on him, so Rob would have to pay the cover charge himself. Rob was annoyed but paid the $40 cover charge for both. Seated at the desk was an old man in casual clothes.

Inside the bar, it was jammed packed. The slave boy auction always brought out a heavy turnout. Most of the men were dressed casually for a leather bar. There were a few men wearing rubber shirts and pants. A few men were also in leather harnesses, black leather G-strings, black caps, and black Army work boots. A stage was set up near the entrance to the bar. On stage was a middle-aged woman holding a microphone and a whip.

"Hello, everybody, and welcome to our eleventh annual slave boy auction. My name is Wendy, and I'm your hostess for tonight. We have some of the cutest boys here for your approval. First out tonight is Jim," Wendy said.

Jim stepped onto the stage. He wore a black leather harness, a black cap, black Army work boots, and a black leather G-string that did not cover his pubic hair. He was fat. No one wanted to "buy" him. Several people in the bar started to boo at Jim. Soon, just about everybody in the bar was booing at Jim. Jim was crestfallen. He stepped off the stage onto the floor. Then he went to a wall, put his arm against the wall, and started to cry. This was the most humiliating night of his life.

"Not to worry. We have more pulchritudinous pups backstage. And they're just dyin' to come out on stage. Who's our next contestant?" Wendy asked.

Backstage, a shy, slightly built, boyish-looking guy named Mike stood nervously. He had signed up for the slave boy auction looking for a father figure. However, this was turning into more than he had bargained for. The bar owner had ordered him to put on a leather G-string, a leather harness, and a leather cap. He felt mortified and embarrassed.

"Do I have to go out like this?" Mike asked the bar's owner.

"Look, son, you came to me looking for a daddy. Now get your cute little boy ass out there, and find a daddy!" the bar owner ordered.

Mike did as he was told but with foreboding.

Mike came out. However, in comparison to Tim, he looked angelic.

"Who would want this little cutie for a slave? What is our first bid? One hundred dollars?" Wendy cried out.

One hundred, someone in the crowd yelled out. Two hundred, someone else cried out. These cries soon were met with a $300 bid, then a $500 bid. Rob was looking out at this with disgust. What is wrong with these guys? This is sick, Rob thought.

Richard Jordan wanted Mike to take him back to his lair.

"That boy is spank bait," Richard said.

Richard ordered Rob to "buy" the boy. Rob did not want to do this but had to stay on Richard's good side, so he "bid" $600 for the boy.

"Maybe we'll hit a thousand for little Mikie," Wendy said.

All this mortified Mike. All these men were hooting, hollering, and whistling at Mike's cute body. Wendy ordered Mike to turn around. When the crowd saw MIke's adorable little boy butt, they let out a roar. The men were using their cell phones to photograph Mike. The group was drunk, loud, rowdy, and horny. This was more than Mike could stand. He was embarrassed to tears. He did not know that many horny drunk men would treat him like a piece of meat. He fled from the stage.

Backstage, the bar owner grabbed Mike by his hair.

"Look, boy, you came to me lookin' for a daddy. You're not keepin' your word. You signed a contract to appear in this auction. Do you see that stockade over there? The bar owner pointed to some stockades backstage. That's where you're goin' if you don't get back on that stage, now, boy!" the bar owner barked.

The bar owner motioned for two burly bodyguards to take Mike back onstage. Mike tried to resist, but he was no match for the bodyguards.

As he was brought back onstage, Wendy said:

"Here comes back, Mikie. Can anybody say 'bad boy'? Can anyone say spanking?"

Wendy then cracked the whip she was holding.

Mike stood there silently as the bodyguards held him in place and started to cry. This was the most humiliating night of his life.

"How much do you have on you?" Robert Jordan asked Rob.

Rob had a thousand dollars on him, but he wanted that for rent and groceries.

"I have a thousand," Rob said.

"Bid it on, Mike," Richard Jordan ordered.

A thousand dollars on a slave boy! Rob thought.

"Do you want a part in my next film," Richard asked.

Rob did as he was told; a part, even a small one, in a Richard Jordan production could jump-start his career.

He walked up to the stage and shouted:

"A thousand dollars!

The crowd went quiet at this bid.

"A thousand dollars! Do you hear that? Do I hear eleven hundred dollars?" Wendy cried out.

When there were no competing bids, Wendy cried out:

"A thousand dollars, going once, going twice, going three times. Sold to the gentlemen in the audience. Go down to the gentlemen in the audience," Wendy said to Mike.

Mike stepped down off the stage, and Rob walked up to him. Rob paid the thousand dollars at a table next to the stage. Rob put his hand on Mike's shoulder and said reassuringly:

"It's okay. Just go get dressed and come back here."

Rob could not wait to get away from these sickos. They made his skin crawl.

Mike came back fully dressed. Rob took him by the hand and helped him navigate the crowd back to Richard Jordan. Some of the men in the group were taking photos of Mike. Several of the men made passes at Mike by either pinching or patting his buttocks or just letting their hands slide across Mike's chest. Mike felt thoroughly humiliated by their attentions. He did not like being treated like a piece of meat. Every man in that crowd wished that he had won the bid for Mike. That was how cute Mike was.

A sadomasochist organization was running the slave boy auction. They collected the money for the "slave boys." Rob told Mike that tonight was Mike's lucky night.

"Do you know whom you're going to meet tonight? You're going to meet Richard Jordan tonight.

When they reached Richard, Richard cried out:

"Be still my heart. Look at you. You're so cute," Richard gushed.

"Do you want to get in the movies, little boy?" Richard Jordan asked Mike.

Mike couldn't get into films after he had been in a slave boy auction, but Mike did not know that. Richard could lead Mike on with promises of stardom, just like he led all the teenage male prostitutes he used and then threw away. Rob and Mike were no exception. Richard was biding his time until he could use and throw away Rob and Mike. Richard had what he wanted for the night. Before they left, though, Richard set some ground rules.

"You will call me sir, boy," Richard said to Mike.

Rob rolled his eyes. He could not believe how arrogant and self-important Richard was acting.

The three of them left the bar. They got in Richard Jordan's car and headed back to Bel Air. The tension had been so thick on the way over here, and on the way back, it was just as tense. Rob could not wait to get this evening over with. On the one hand, he could not stand Richard Jordan.

On the other hand, Richard Jordan could make or break him. So he had to try to stay on Richard's good side. They arrived at Richard's Bel Air mansion high in the Hollywood Hills. They all went into Richard's estate.

"Who wants a drink?" Richard asked as they walked into the living room.

Rob and Mike both said that they would like a drink. Rob thought that he could use a drink.

Richard went to his portable bar on the side of the living room. The mobile bar had two shelves on it. Richard placed the glasses on the lower shelf. That way, he could spike the drinks, and Rob and Mike would not see what he was doing. He mixed the drinks, but he did not drug the drinks. That would come later. Then he walked over to Rob and Mike and handed them their drinks.

Then Richard said to Mike:

"Let's see what ya got, strip!" Richard ordered.

Mike was surprised. He had not expected to be asked to strip so quickly.

"Well, are you willing to do nude scenes, or aren't you?" Richard demanded.

"Yes," Mike answered haltingly.

"Well, then strip," Richard ordered.

Rob rolled his eyes. This dirty old man was taking advantage of this barely legal young man. Mike was mortified, but he did as he was told. He stripped under Richard's intense gaze. Richard enjoyed every minute of this. When Mike had stripped, Richard ordered him to turn around. Mike turned around.

"Not bad, not bad at all. Now I want to see you all wet. Go out to the pool. You too, Rob. I want to see both of you in the pool," Richard said.

Mike, Rob, and Richard went back to the pool. Mike walked into the pool. Richard turned to Rob.

"You, too, strip and get in the pool," Richard ordered.

Rob rolled his eyes. He did not like to be ordered around, but Richard held the upper hand. Rob stripped and went into the pool. Rob and Mike swam past each other a couple of times.

"Okay, now I want an audition from both of you. I want some man-on-man action. If you want to break into films, you're going to have to hug other men. I want both of you facing each other," Richard said.

Mike and Rob faced each other.

"Now Mike, I want you to massage Rob's chest. Now, Rob, I want you to lick Mike's ear," Richard ordered.

That did it! Rob had had enough!

"That does it! I am not going to paw this boy for your sick fantasies. The audition ends now!" Rob shouted.

Rob put his hand on Mike's shoulder and said:

"It's all right. Go back in the house and get dressed."

Mike was relieved. This whole evening was becoming more bizarre than he had counted on. As he walked past Richard, Richard said:

"Blacklist, blacklist."

Richard was referring to the infamous blacklist.

"Once I put you on the blacklist, you're as good as dead. You'll never work again. No one put on the blacklist is ever taken off it again," Richard said.

"This is enough. That boy has vulnerability written all across his face. He's looking for someone to protect him, and you and those sickos at that bar are taking advantage of him, and it ends right now! I don't care what you do to me, but you will not take advantage of that boy!" Rob shouted.

"He's over twenty-one. He's a consenting adult. He consented to pose nude. I'm not taking advantage of anyone," Richard said as he held his drink aloft.

Richard's aloof manner only infuriated Rob.

"We're goin' back in the house," Rob said.

Rob got dressed, and he and Richard went back into the house. Now was the time to use the date rape drugs, Richard decided.

Richard spiked the drinks at the bar, and Rob and Mike would not see what he was doing. He put the powdered date rape drugs in Rob's and Mike's drinks and walked over to them. Mike had gotten dressed by now. Richard handed him his drink while holding Rob's drink in his other hand. Rob was instantly suspicious. He did not trust Richard by now.

"Don't drink that, Mike," Rob said.

Richard and Mike looked at Rob.

"What did you put in that drink?" Rob asked.

"Nothing, nothing at all," Richard answered.

"Then you drink it," Rob ordered.

Richard did not dare drink the drink.

"You don't give the orders in my house!" Richard growled back.

" Don't drink that drink, Mike," Rob ordered Mike.

Rob said he wanted to be paid before anything went further.

"I'll pay the money when I'm good and ready! Here's your drink. Do as I say, you goddamned little cunt!!!

Rob did not remember lifting his fist. However, before Rob knew it, he punched Richard Jordan in the nose. Rob knocked

Richard Jordan to the ground and then sat on Richard Jordan's chest. He continued to pummel Richard in the face, giving Richard two black eyes and a bloody nose.

Rob had had enough of Richard Jordan.

"You call me up. You act as if you own me! I've had all I'm going to take from you! I want my money, and I want it now!" Rob screamed at Richard.

"I don't have it!" Richard replied with terror in his voice.

"You don't have it!?!" Rob shouted at Richard.

Then he pummeled his fists against Richard's nose and eyes even harder.

Then Rob stood up and started for the door. He took Mike by the hand and said:

"C'mon, we're outta here."

Before he reached the door, he heard Richard say:

"You're finished. You're finished. You'll never work in this town! You goddamned little cunt!!

Upon hearing the word cunt, Rob turned around and went over to Richard and pummeled him again. Finally, Richard begged Rob to stop. At this point, Rob stopped. He then walked to the front door, and he heard Richard say:

"You're finished in this town. I have a lot of power, and I'll ensure you never work in this town again!" "You're on the blacklist as of now!"

Rob went out the front door and walked to the street with Mike. He thought about what Richard Jordan had told him and realized he would never be hired as an actor after tonight. This was the end of his dreams. All he had ever wanted was to be a star. And now, that dream was over. He did not know what he would do for the rest of his life. Yet he did not have the energy to think about that now. He and Mike started walking back to Sunset Boulevard. A security guard gave them a ride back down to Sunset. From there, they took a cab to Hollywood. He gave Mike a ride to Mike's apartment and said goodbye to him. He would never see Mike again.

He wondered how he would support his wife and baby after tonight. When he got home, he stripped and crawled beside his wife. He fitfully tried to fall asleep, but it was not easy tonight.

Meanwhile, back at Richard Jordan's house, he phoned John and told him:

"I have a job for you! Call your low-life friends. I want you to throw some acid in a pretty boy's face."

Richard Jordan would have his revenge.

One thing, though, Richard did not know Rob's address. Richard told John to get that address pronto. John did not know the address, but for Richard Jordan, he promised that he would get it. John called Steve, who had thrown the party yesterday. John told Steve that Richard Jordan wanted Rob's address. John let it slip that Richard Jordan wanted to throw acid in Rob's face. Steve was aghast about this. Steve could not afford to displease Richard Jordan because Richard Jordan was so powerful. However, Steve did not have Rob's address. For that, John hired the private detective to the stars. The private detective would take a day to track Rob's address from his cell phone number. Before then, Steve telephoned Rob.

When Rob answered the phone, he heard the voice of Steve.

"Dear boy, don't hang up. I've got some terrible news for you. Richard Jordan is going to try to throw some acid in your face. You sure made some powerful enemies! You've got to get out of town immediately. You have to get out of Dodge before it's too late. They can track you down from your cell phone number! You still have a little time to get away. Save yourself before it's too late. Get out of town now!!!" Steve would never hear from Rob again.

Rob was thunderstruck by this turn of events. He had been soundly asleep when this phone call came in. Now he was wide awake and upset. This was utterly sadistic. He immediately realized that he would have to leave Los Angeles immediately. The first order of business was to get his wife and baby out of harm's way. He turned to Sheila and told her to get up. They would have to leave. His wife was a sound sleeper, and she was very groggy. She asked him why they had to leave all of a sudden. Rob told her that he would explain later. Just now, get dressed quickly so we can leave here pronto. Sheila did as she was asked, and she dressed quickly. She then took the baby, sleeping in her bassinet, and carried out the baby while taking a big purse with her. The bag contained diapers and baby formula. Then the three of them got in their car and went to a motel on Sunset Boulevard. When they entered the motel room, Sheila asked him about this moving suddenly.

"All right, do you want to tell me why we've left our apartment for this seedy motel room?" Sheila asked.

Rob would have to think quickly on his feet. He could not let Sheila know that he had been a gigolo. He would have to make up a story. He decided to tell her that one of his catering gigs had gone awry and that he was being targeted for acid in his face by one of the most powerful men in Hollywood.

"Look, at this catering gig, Richard Jordan got angry at me and threatened to throw acid in my face," Rob said.

"Why would he throw acid in your face?" Sheila asked incredulously.

"Because he's a sadistic, spiteful, poor excuse for a human being. That's why." Rob said.

So how is he going to find you?" Sheila asked.

"He has enough connections that he can find out where we live. That's why we've got to go into hiding for a little while," Rob answered.

All this turning of events nonplused Sheila.

"Well, how long will we be hiding?" she asked.

"I can't say how long. It'll just have to be for a little while until this Richard Jordan guy gives up on finding us," Rob said.

Sheila was upset. First, she had been roused from a sound sleep, and now she was being told that they would have to live in hiding. She was exhausted, and she wanted to go back to sleep. Rob told her to go back to sleep. In the meantime, he would return to the apartment and pack as much stuff as he could. Richard Jordan's henchmen would not have found Rob's address so quickly. Rob still had a few hours to get their belongings and leave Dodge.

Rob returned to the apartment. In the apartment, he grabbed as many clothes out of the closet as he could carry and put the clothes in the car's back seat. Then he emptied the dresser drawers and put those clothes in the car's back seat. Then he went back into the apartment. He could not fit the bassinet into the backseat of the car. It would have to stay behind. So would the pots and pans have to stay behind too? However, he could collect the baby's toys and take a big box of Pamper's diapers.

Rob was nervous and anxious as he packed up everything he could and put it in the backseat of the car. Son, the county doesn't pay us to send you out on dates, he heard one of his voices say. He could not cope with voices today. He wished the voices would go away.

After Rob packed the car, he decided to go to Las Vegas. He had not left a forwarding address at his apartment, so tracing him to Las Vegas would be difficult. Gotta keep movin', he thought.

A day later, Richard Jordan's henchmen arrived at Rob's apartment. They walked up to his apartment. They jimmied the lock with a master key for apartment houses. They did not see Rob taking clothes and baby toys when they went inside. They did not know that Rob had fled only a day sooner. The apartment looked like someone was living in it. They decided to stay there until Rob came back. They would have a long wait. Rob was way ahead of them. They would never find him. After several months, Richard Jordan stopped looking for him. At this point, he could relax. Rob picked up his wife and baby from the motel. They had to keep on moving until they reached Las Vegas. Then they could relax a little. Rob had about $10,000 in cash on him from his prostitution work. They could live off that for a couple of months. That would give Rob time to enroll in bartender school. He could get a job as a bartender at one of the casinos. This would give him a middle-class lifestyle and a way to support his wife and baby. After a few months, the threats from Richard Jordan would all seem like a bad dream. He would build a new life in Las Vegas. Son, the county doesn't pay us to send you out on dates, he heard his voices say as he drove off to his new life in Las Vegas. Son, the county doesn't pay us to send you out on dates.

For the next year, Rob lived his life while looking over his shoulder. He left no trace of his escape to Las Vegas. However, they could find him if someone wanted to spend enough money. After a year, without any incidents, he finally settled down to his new life peacefully. Although he still heard voices with his wife and daughter and a steady job at one of the casinos, he led as normal a life as was possible for someone with schizophrenia. He almost lived happily ever after.

Son, the county doesn't pay us to send you out on dates.
THE END